HOPE SPRINGS ETERNAL: AN ANTHOLOGY OF HOPEFUL POETRY

Edited with an Introduction by J. R. Simons

J. R. Simons
John Burroughs
Amanda Hayden
Joseph Balaz
Jessica Weyer Bentley
Christen Lee
Ashley Pacholewski
Barbara Sabol
A. Garnett Weiss
Sandra Rivers-Gill
Joel Lipman
Thomas Barden
LaVern Spencer McCarthy

Emily Jane VandenBos Style
J. V. Sadler
Julie Marie Hoey

Simple Simons Press

Copyright © 2023 Simple Simons Press

All rights reserved

All poems in this collection are reprinted with the express written consent of the authors, and they retain all other subsidiary rights in their work(s). Reprint rights revert back to the authors upon publication of this collection.

The characters and events portrayed in this book are fictitious. Any similarity to real persons, living or dead, is coincidental and not intended by the author.

No part of this book may be reproduced, or stored in a retrieval system, or transmitted in any form or by any means, electronic, mechanical, photocopying, recording, or otherwise, without express written permission of the publisher.

Cover design by: J.R. Simons

Printed in the United States of America

CONTENTS

Title Page
Copyright
Introduction
Snoetry Invocation — 1
This World is Loud (Watching Ukraine) — 3
Good Advice — 6
A Softening Vow — 8
New Moon — 10
Fireworks from Forest Fires — 12
After Elizabeth Bishop — 14
Summer along the Stonycreek — 16
Under The Bodhi Tree — 18
The Lotus — 20
Love — 22
After listening to numerous complaints of no room of my own — 24
Time in the hourless houses — 26
About the Looks at the Oscars — 28
Janie — 30
Downstate Ticket — 31
It Didn't Matter — 34

Another Attempt to Make Hard-Boiled Eggs	36
Landing	38
Among The Ruins	40
Heavenly Conversation	42
After The Storm	44
Cellphone Reach	45
I write this poem in the dark	46
The Sea Tamer	47
Cool Definite	49
A Hopeful World	50
Rhythms	51
Gatha	53
In the Wake	54
Cleanse	55
Books By This Author	59

INTRODUCTION

An Essay on (Hu)man(ity)

> Hope humbly then; with trembling pinions soar;
> Wait the great teacher Death; and God adore!
> What future bliss, he gives not thee to know,
> But gives that hope to be thy blessing now.
> Hope springs eternal in the human breast:
> Man never is, but always to be blest:
> The soul, uneasy and confin'd from home,
> Rests and expatiates in a life to come.
> • Alexander Pope, "An Essay on Man: Epistle I" (1733)

Is hope a boon or a bane to humanity? Ancient Greek mythology seems to paint it as both, and both interpretations are bound up in the myths of Prometheus and Pandora. Prometheus gave man the gift of fire; therefore, making them like the gods. For this, he was punished, chained to the mountainside where vultures would eat his liver daily only for it to grow back overnight and be devoured again the next day. For this, too, man was punished, with Zeus creating the first woman, Pandora, gifting her with a jar filled with all evils and telling her not to open the jar under any circumstances, but she did.

Hope plays an important part in both of these myths. In the myth of Prometheus (Forethought), fire is the second gift he gives to man; the first is hope. In *Prometheus Bound*, one of Aeschylus' great tragedies, Prometheus tells the chorus how he has benefitted man with his gifts:

> Chorus: Did you perhaps go further than you have told us?
> Prometheus: I stopped mortals from foreseeing their fate.
> Chorus: What kind of cure did you discover for this sickness?
> Prometheus: I established in them blind hopes.
> Chorus: This is a great benefit you gave to men.

According to Aeschylus, "blind hopes" are a "great benefit to men," for with blind hopes, men may never see their own fate, the fate that Plato proposes in the Er myth at the end of *Republic* – that the just are rewarded and the wicked are punished. To know one's own fate is to live a potentially tortured existence, should one know they will be punished, or to live a potentially entitled existence, should one know they will be rewarded. However, not knowing one's fate, one can live in the "blind hopes" that they will be rewarded for being just.

In Hesiod's story of Pandora, she is fashioned by the gods to beguile men, to be the beautiful dread that all men long for. She is sent by Zeus to Epimetheus (Afterthought) who ignores or forgets Prometheus' warning not to accept gifts from Zeus and who takes her as his wife. Soon, Pandora opens a storage jar in their home, also said to be a gift from Zeus, releasing into the world all the toils, tribulations, struggles, and strifes it contained as a reminder to man that Zeus was the creator of their lives and in control of their fates and destinies. Pandora closes the jar leaving only one evil trapped within – a timid sprite named Elpis, variously translated as "hope" or "expectation." For Hesiod, hope, or perhaps more accurately, expectation, is an evil best kept locked up in the jar. Perhaps this kind of hope is better referred to as false hope, the kind of false hope, or high hopes, "that make that little old ant think he can move a rubber tree plant." Hesiod's hope, or rather expectation, is a trick, which makes men believe they are more than what they actually are, that they are entitled to favor because they have expectations of favor. Perhaps these high hopes are best kept locked in the jar forever because they breed pride.

Expectation, then, is the mythical evil of hope, that which Pandora kept locked in the jar. For with expectation, man grows proud, and it is pride that leads to all manner of evil, as Pope goes on to say in Canto V of *An Essay on Man: Epistle I* –

> Ask for what end the heav'nly bodies shine,
> Earth for whose use? Pride answers, " 'Tis for mine:
> For me kind Nature wakes her genial pow'r,
> Suckles each herb, and spreads out ev'ry flow'r;
> Annual for me, the grape, the rose renew,
> The juice nectareous, and the balmy dew;
> For me, the mine a thousand treasures brings;
> For me, health gushes from a thousand springs;
> Seas roll to waft me, suns to light me rise;
> My foot-stool earth, my canopy the skies."

Therefore, hope is double-edged sword – at once blinding humanity to its fate and allowing individuals to have a modicum of peace in the hope that they might enjoy a favorable fate in the afterlife while also being the bane of humanity's existence as it builds pride in men whose high hopes grant them the expectation of rewards. Sound familiar?

Conversely, hope may be the only thing we have left, and hope is something we must hang onto fiercely as we attempt to navigate the seemingly hopeless dystopian future that awaits us.

I've asked poets to share angry poems for *Mad As Hell: An Anthology of Angry Poems*, and now I've asked poets to share hopeful poems for *Hope Springs Eternal: An Anthology of Hopeful Poetry*. Little did I know what to expect when poets, left to their own devices, submitted poems describing their versions of "hope." There is no way to shape this anthology; it shaped itself as themes emerged with each poem.

The meaning of "hope" is defined differently by each one. In this little volume, you will find a multitude of meanings and interpretations, including –

Amanda Hayden's admonition to

> dive low into your deep pockets
> of hope folded and unfolded
> because this damaged world is loud
> but our bruised, tender hearts can be louder

Joseph Balaz's "Good Advice" –

> to make an effort
> to amass your stones
>
> so you can be ready
> when the time comes
>
> to take on Goliath.

Jessica Weyer Bentley's "the sun'll come out tomorrow" belief that –

> We all are swords of unwavering hope,
> striking hard against the grim frozen world,
> ushering in a humble but gleaming chance
> that shadow will always give rise to daybreak.

And my favorite line in the entire collection from Barbara Sabol -

> Listen now to the river's patter, reminding us
> not everything is broken.

Pope tells us that "Hope springs eternal in the human breast" and tells us that there is a better world coming in the afterlife. The poets contained in this little volume, however, tell us that the better world of the afterlife can be had here on earth if we want it. The Apostle Paul tells us that "Faith, Hope, and Love abide, but the greatest of these is Love," a sentiment echoed in all the hopeful poetry in this volume, but perhaps best stated by Ashley Pacholewski –

> Love will laugh and
> remind you that
> we suffer to get well,
> we surrender to win,
> we die to live,
> and we give it away to keep it.

In a world so meanly disposed, weary of an unending and unwinnable war against terrorism, ravaged by a global pandemic, plagued by fear, and slouching its way toward Armageddon, can poets be its last best hope for peace?

JR Simons, Editor
Publisher
Simple Simons Press

> In giving freedom to the slave, we assure freedom to the free - honorable alike in what we give, and what we preserve. We shall nobly save, or meanly lose, the last best hope of earth.
> • Abraham Lincoln, Address to Congress (1862)

SNOETRY INVOCATION

By John Burroughs

Snoetry Invocation

by John Burroughs

Come ye, poets
from far and close
for this is the day
the lowered have made.

Let us resurrect
the spring of our words
the summer of our steps
the fall and response
of the why'd world
the wild whirled sorts
of the way fairer
and let us rejoice
and let us repeat
rejoice.

Let us look up
and thank the stars
as creative beings would
for this is the day
and it is good.

Let us rejoice
though we have
been the lowered
and let us rise up
to greet the gray snow
and great glad sun
and kiss the ghost
of Hermann Hesse
exhaling his blessing
on grateful concrete
embrace the pregnant
cinderblock and blow
our noses like holy cornets
in celebration of the hour
and our impending ascension

❊ ❊ ❊

John Burroughs of Cleveland was recently selected as the 2022-2023 U.S. Beat Poet Laureate and previously served for two years as Ohio's Beat Poet Laureate. He is the author of *Rattle & Numb: Selected and New Poems, 1992-2019* [2019, Venetian Spider] and more than a dozen chapbooks. John has curated several regular reading series in the Greater Cleveland area and currently moderates the northeast Ohio literary calendar at clevelandpoetry.com. Since 2008 has served as the founding editor of Crisis Chronicles Press, publishing 120 titles and counting by vital independent voices from across the U.S. and beyond. Find him at crisischronicles.com.

THIS WORLD IS LOUD (WATCHING UKRAINE)

by Amanda Hayden

this world is loud
a percussion of restless tongues
our thoughts are loud
     rowdy, flawed, and exhausting

here is an invitation
to remember we are more
than this unfiltered chaos
     than our compulsive inner spiraling

more than restless observers
more than misguided motivation
more than perpetual checklists
     and endless pressure of completion

collectively, we watch, and we wait
a stunning David push back a relentless Goliath
 watch compulsively, intensively, helplessly
     as insulated voyeurs

because we know
this could be us; this could be us
and we have to ask, would we have this grit
     this unwavering resistance

against such terror
and insatiable snuffing of life
against such desensitized destruction
    and cloaked fury

what is there to do
but sing our mourning songs
and estranged praises
    with our clumsy protests and cracked wings

what is there to do
but refuse to ever ignore
Hey, what's that sound
    and hold vigil for what is in shreds

what is there to do
except to look at each other wholly
and utter my God, my God
    as the psalmists did

to whisper my humanity, my humanity
if we just had today
what would you be anchored by
    what sun would turn your face toward

what would you give away without hesitation
what precious words would you choose
and who would you give them to
    if we just had today

would you be a mirror
or a catalyst
in stillness, in focus
    on your heart, your heart

when the rock and rubble slide and break
you dig into your edged truth
stretch and reach down into

>   your exposed gnarled roots

dive low into your deep pockets
of hope folded and unfolded
because this damaged world is loud
>   but our bruised, tender hearts can be

>   louder

❋ ❋ ❋

Hayden is Poet Laureate for Sinclair College and Professor of Humanities, Philosophy, and Religions (emphasis in Indigenous, Eastern, and Environmental Studies), receiving several pedagogy awards, including the SOCHE Award (2017) and the League for Innovation Teaching Excellence Award (2020). Her chapter, "Saunter Like Muir: Experience Projects in Environmental Ethics" was recently published by Routledge (2022) in *Eco pedagogies: Practical Approaches to Experiential Learning*. She also pub lished a book of stories: *Windy Chicken Farm Animal Rescue*. She lives with her family on a small farm with three dogs, two cats, two goats, seven pigs, many chickens, and a duck named Dorothy.

GOOD ADVICE

by Joseph Balaz

I am aware of Finland's stand
against the Soviet Union in 1939,

the college basketball win
by Chaminade against Virginia in 1982,

Morris the Florist's

battle against tyrannical trucking
companies in *The Pushcart War,*

Sir Richard Branson's inability
to read at the age of 11

and being bounced around
between schools for low grades

until he eventually scored bigtime,

who Hiram
the ordinary housefly became

when he put those cool glasses on,

and what Cinderella
had to go through

to get to where she got.

So if there's
any good advice to give

it's to make an effort
to amass your stones

so you can be ready
when the time comes

to take on Goliath.

❋ ❋ ❋

Joe Balaz writes in American English and in Hawaiian Islands Pidgin (HIP). He is a writer, visual artist, and freelance improv musician, who has created works in poetry, visual poetry, and music poetry. Balaz has been published in Hawai'i and Ohio, as well as nationally and internationally. He is the author of Pidgin Eye, a book of poetry, and he is also the editor of 13 Miles from Cleveland. a literary and art magazine. Balaz presently lives in Cleveland, Ohio.

A SOFTENING VOW

by Jessica Weyer Bentley

In the icy February sunrise,
the snowfall hardens from the frozen harshness,
the vista full of darkened gray,
and the birds too chilled to sing,
the dreary sky mirrors a frozen pond.
In a flash of oblique stillness an organic
hue of spring cuts the wake of winter's plane,
offering the anticipation of warm breezes,
jubilation,
holding rough hands in salty air.
Promise is but a single blade.
We all are swords of unwavering hope,
striking hard against the grim frozen world,
ushering in a humble but gleaming chance
that shadow will always give rise to daybreak.

❋ ❋ ❋

Jessica Weyer Bentley is an Author/Poet. Her first collection of poetry, *Crimson Sunshine*, was published in May 2020 by AlyBlue Media. She has contributed work to several publications for the Award-Winning Book Series, Grief Diaries, including *Poetry and Prose*, and *Hit by a Drunk Driver*. Jessica's work has been anthologized in *Women Speak Vol. 6* (Sheila-Na-Gig Editions), *Summer Gallery of Shoes* (Highland Park Poetry), *Common Threads 2020 Edition* (Ohio Poetry Association), *Appalachian Witness Volume 24* and *Appalachian Unmasked Volume 25* (Pine Mountain Sand and Gravel) and *Made and Dream* (Of Rust and Glass), 2021 and online blogs including *Global Poemic*, *Lothlorian Poetry Journal* and *Fevers of the Mind* and many other anthologies, magazines, and journals. She is currently penning her second collection of poetry, *Down Below Where the Canary Sings*, slated for publication in Spring 2023 by The Sage Owl Publishing. Jessica currently resides in Northwest Ohio.

NEW MOON

by Christen Lee

Three nights after the new moon,
I search the sky for what's almost not there.
You can just make out that thread of white
piercing the black
like a needling comma,

A pause,
while the world continues
counting days and moons,
years cycling the burning sun
on this earth with its birthing and dying
and everything that fills the in between.

But tonight it's spring
and nearly alive
on this green stretch of possibility.
See how hope pokes through,
soft shoots rise up
to face the waxing moon.

Of course it's only natural
to fall in love with what's born
and to suffer what's lost.
And it's so easy to feel time's gravity
in the thick blood dusk,
the night closing in like a lover's goodbye

leaving us tilted on earth's axis
and spinning toward ruin.

Look at the bird with the broken wing
lying motionless under the nesting oak.
And I think, at least he knew that rapture of flight
out here in this sacred space.
And in this way I bargain my sadness
on and on.
We spend our days threading
new ways through joys and sorrows
on and on.

So I root for the moon to spot me
thread me back onto the solid ground.
How I need a silver lining
that cosmic life line to steady me
in this giant empty
that reaches on and on
as far as the eye can believe.

❋ ❋ ❋

Christen Lee is a family nurse practitioner in Cleveland, Ohio. Her writing has been featured or is forthcoming in Literary Cleveland's *Voices from the Edge Anthology, Rue Scribe, The Write Launch, Aurora, Humans of the World Blog, Sad Girls Club, 2022 New Generation Beats Anthology, Wingless Dreamer, The Voices of Real 7 Compilation, Ariel Chart,* and *The Elevation Review.*

FIREWORKS FROM FOREST FIRES

by Ashley Pacholewski

More than the ruby blooms rising
Out of forest fire ashes–
More than the fluttering of petals
Like butterflies and their kissing wings–
It's the patience of the seedlings I adore.

When sacred Cypress soaked up sun,
The grounded seeds laid peacefully,
Living in their present moments
Until circumstances allowed for Light
To kiss the ground and invite
Sprouts to tip-toe above the Earth
And stay awhile.

Those fire flowers delighted in the dark,
But stayed curious enough to
Adventure and treasure a place
Beyond their imaginations
Where they were borne again.

❋ ❋ ❋

Ashley Pacholewski is a teacher that enjoys reading poetry, watercolor painting, and running. She lives in Medina, Ohio with her husband and two little guys, Leo and Oliver. She has previously published poems in *Storms of the Inland Sea: Poems of Alzheimer's and Dementia Caregiving* (2022), Cleveland's Hessler Street Fair Anthologies (2015, 2018), and Ohio Poetry Association's *Best of 2020*. In her spare time, she loves writing poems of her own, laughing, and being silly with her kids.

AFTER ELIZABETH BISHOP

by Christen Lee

The great poet once said,
"The art of losing isn't hard to master."
And I've lived in poems
in lines
closed in on the ends,
I've lost my way.
On any given day
the world is full of metaphors
for loss.

It's easy to sink low.
God, I could spend days
building shrines
to the past,
mourning shadows
of the living,
but the art of finding is also worth mastering,
even necessary,
I would argue.

Look, see this soft, cool earth
from aching knees
dark soil

soft blades of grass
bleed hope plead
find me feel me
breeze these hands
with words in bands
of sun
until I can say,
it is well where I am.

Listen to the sounds of sweetness
my children call me
oh this urgent happiness.

The lost kitten comes home
purrs purrs
look we've all made it.
We are found
by one another.

❋ ❋ ❋

SUMMER ALONG THE STONYCREEK

by Barbara Sabol

From a needle eye in the Alleghenies
this sheet of liquid shimmer
unseams the earth.

Steel rail and forest trail
run alongside, north and west
to the Highlands.

The current circles, carves, deepens
for the child's cannonball,
the raccoon's cupped hands,
ribbon snake's undulation,
a polished assembly of stars.

See how the water gathers
oak's shadow, hemlock's needled brush
in its wending,

how the shifting clouds and lift
of broad-winged hawk echo
on its surface.

Intimate of the weathered ridges
that tender stones meant for skipping
the long-cast width.

One with sky, river meets itself
as deluge, thin rain, as mist.

A body could float through time
on its muscled back -- in its depths
our stories are ferried: caravan
of arrowhead, latchkey, crockery, bone.

Listen now to the river's patter, reminding us
not everything is broken.

❄ ❄ ❄

"Summer along the Stonycreek" was first published in *I Thought I Heard a Cardinal Sing: Ohio's Appalachian Voices*.

❄ ❄ ❄

Barbara Sabol is a retired speech pathologist who carries on her love affair with language through poetry. Her fifth collection, *CONNECTIONS: core & all—haiku and senryu*, was published by Bird Dog Press in 2022. She is the associate editor of *Sheila-Na-Gig* online, and edited the 2022 anthology, *Sharing this Delicate Bread: Selections from Sheila-Na-Gig online*.

Her awards include an Individual Excellence Award from the Ohio Arts Council. Barbara conducts poetry workshops through Literary Cleveland. She lives in Akron, Ohio with her husband and two wonder dogs.

UNDER THE BODHI TREE

by Joseph Balaz

Getting ethereal
can be a prelude to the spiritual

because there's so much to grasp

in the reasoning
of what you are contemplating.

Inevitably though,

it does seem
to be beyond reach

in the reaching for it.

Imagine if a goldfish
could talk

and you asked the scaly creature,

"Do you believe in God?

Maybe the observing fish
might tell you,

"I'm not sure,

*but I hope that food keeps falling
out of the sky for me."*

That response is just as good,

as any other speculation
I've heard on the matter,

in pondering the unseen force
that is holding everything together.

As for me
I'm still randomly searching,

and day to day
sometimes I go back and forth

with different notions.

Just like Buddha
sitting under the Bodhi tree,

there's always more ways

to try and explore
your existence in the world.

THE LOTUS

by Christen Lee

My brain suffers from a chemical imbalance
that leaves me starving for happiness.
And it's not just me.
My mother, my father,
my mother's mother and father,
my father's father and mother
suffered too.
Which is to say that we are a sad progeny
whose tears span our lineage.

But it's not all despair.
It's been said, how can one appreciate the light
until experiencing the great dark.

Well, I've spent half my life in the shadows
straining for a glimmer.
And would you believe that I have trained myself
to see through darkness?
To imagine all the things illuminated by day:
the sun with its warm promise,
the trees with their gentle sway,
the earth with its cool, firm footing?

And would you believe that I have set my mind to task,
placed one sure hand after another
and scaled these subterranean walls?

THE LOTUS

Yes, I have seen the brilliant light of day.
I have emerged from the labyrinth
from which I was born.

One thing I will tell you.
Once met by the light of the living,
the thick cover of night recedes.
The soul rises
and opens like a lotus,
exposing its radiant splendor
for all the world to see.

This is how a lotus is born.

LOVE

by Ashley Pacholewski

Before you know what love really is
you must grieve things,
feel the emptiness a loss leaves
like the coldness that lays on you after a fire smolders.
The hand you were holding, the comfort of connection
turns to nothing but air
while what is left of life lays in the ground.
You must know the depth of valleys
that gave birth to the highest peaks of mountains.
You must descend and descend
into the bottom of the human heart,
craving the light that has become stardust.

Before you learn the ethereal levity of love
you must watch a mother insatiably
wail as she refuses to let go of her little lifeless one.
You must see her live her greatest nightmare,
heartbeat watering the seedling inside her,
roots intertwined with delicate veins that recognize
they cannot give more than themselves
for the whimpers and coos of daydreams.

Before you know love as the largest struggle,
you must know indifference as the other struggle.
You must wake up, battling the concept of purpose

and wander the desert for an invisible peace.
When you begin to wonder what lies beyond,
love will let you see the world
and water your heart which will coax it to bloom,
reach for the warmth of sunshine,
perfume the air with pollen,
invite bees to stay,
be merry,
have nectar,
and attract the attention
of those looking for joy.

Love will laugh and
remind you that
we suffer to get well,
we surrender to win,
we die to live,
and we give it away
to keep it.

AFTER LISTENING TO NUMEROUS COMPLAINTS OF NO ROOM OF MY OWN

by Barbara Sabol

my husband marked off the bounds of livable
basement space—2 x 2 furring studs of raw
blond wood —a frame ready for its inspiration.

He heaved unwieldy sheet after sheet of dry wall
down the narrow stairs, sanded, plastered, snugged them
between the beams, over bristly pink insulation,

conjuring private quarters—an island of comfort
within an expanse of grey cement. Until then I could imagine
nothing other than an ordinary, cob-webbed cellar

suitable for dank motors of cooling and heating,
sumps and pipes and whatnots—a domestic dungeon
I'd visit like a pampered survivalist.

Now, a body might escape the overlit upstairs hubbub,
might sink at last into reverie in the polyphonic
underbelly house hum, the unruffled air; here, lit

by a hurricane lamp, at this mission desk. Side walls extend
from a clean white base, a horseshoe-shaped space
welcoming scribbler and scribe, welcoming me—
lucky, lucky.

TIME IN THE HOURLESS HOUSES

by A. Garnett Weiss

We seek a new world through old workings,
correct our watches by the public clocks
where life is a choice of instruments.

Let us stand here and admit we have no road.
(As if a rose could change into a ghost,
and lovers float down from the cliff like rain.)

My senses record the act of wishing
wing-folded peace and eddies of silence
where love was innocent.

I see tomorrow grow a tree of hope,
by the sea's side hear the dark-vowelled birds
and out of nothing, a breathing.

Cento gloss:
Title: Dylan Thomas, "I, In My Intricate Image"
Line 1: Cecil Day Lewis, "As One Who Wanders" (partial line)
Line 2: T.S. Eliot, "Portrait of a Lady"
Line 3: Louis MacNeice, "Sleep, My Body, Sleep, My Ghost" (partial

line)
Line 4: William Empson, "Homage to The British Museum"
Line 5: Edith Sitwell, "Romance"
Line 6: David Gascoyne, "In Defence of Humanism"
Line 7: Stephen Spender, "Never Being, But Always"
Line 8: Ronald Bottrall, "A Grave Revisited"
Line 9: W.H. Auden, "Paysage Moralisé" (partial line)
Line 10: George Baker, "Sacred Elegies, Elegy 1"
Line 11: Dylan Thomas, "Especially When The October Wind"
Line 12: Ezra Pound, "Cantos"
(The title, lines or partial lines, are drawn unaltered, apart from changes in punctuation, from *Twelve Modern Poets*, Editor Artur Lundkvist, The Continental Book Company AB, 1946.)

❦ ❦ ❦

This Canadian's award-winning poetry appears in print and online, either under her name or as A. Garnett Weiss.

Aeolus House published *Bricolage, A Gathering of Centos* (a finalist for the 2022 Fred Kerner Book Award from the Canadian Authors Association), which includes "Time in the hourless houses." *Arc Poetry Magazine* shortlisted the cento for Poem of the Year in 2014. Point Petre Publishing released JC's debut collection, *South Shore Suite...POEMS* (2017).

JC has given workshops for the Ottawa International Writers Festival and Ottawa Public Library, among others. She selects for *byword.ca* and serves on the boards of the Ontario Poetry Society and the Prince Edward Point Bird Observatory. www.jcsulzenko.com.

ABOUT THE LOOKS AT THE OSCARS

by Sandra Rivers-Gill

The winner was read,
and we all gasped.
It still happens, you know --
close ups and smizes captured on film.
On some days we are *just so* . . . .
out-staged, outdressed or un-thanked.
Full of stinging handclaps. Its ok
to wear every feeling all at once.
We don't give up.
Goldenrod gowns have *pink* linings of hope
floating up crystal stairs. It's ok,
who is first on second or third…
We are namers of our own names.
In a ceremony of marveled effects
we are sound makers.
It is what we signed up for --
to cosign ourselves,
and color our craft.
To be a champion
of custom-made worth
is the true calling.
Isn't that the point;

to be seen as lifters --
reshaping ourselves;
representing
forever?

※ ※ ※

An Ohio native, Sandra Rivers-Gill is an award-winning poet, writer, playwright, and performer. She is the editor of a poetry chapbook, "Dopeless Hope Fiends," and recipient of a Toledo Arts Commission Accelerator Grant. Sandra has served as a teaching artist for a treatment facility, drama ministry, senior living communities, and judge for writing competitions. Her work has appeared in or is forthcoming in journals and/or anthologies including; *Hope Springs Eternal, Rise Up Review, North of Oxford, Open Earth III, As It Ought To Be, Poet's Against Racism & Hate USA, Jerry Jazz Musician, ONE ART,* and elsewhere. www.sandrariversgill.com

JANIE

by Jessica Weyer Bentley

What have we grown,
as we have grown old,
our promise in this sun-kissed frame,
never afraid,
pushing hard against this world of asphalt.
She softens it somehow,
revealing a hue of integrity,
of humanity,
in a world angry,
agitated,
brazen in black.
Her aura of seafoam and blue,
breaking through leaving a crack for change.
A mermaid breaking the wake,
revealing herself to the crew.
She rearranges our upbringing,
turning it on its head,
marrying the old and new.
The perfect storm.
Rise up sweet girl.
Take the helm.

DOWNSTATE TICKET

by Joel Lipman

Half the time her guts surged
with "Street Fighting Man,"
the rest, a cued-up earworm
coiled 6 weeks, nerve-wracked jangling
sub-level spinal spiral "…just no place
for, no place for a street fightin'…,"
she'd plug in "girl," chill a pose,
thrust her right arm up
in a revolutionary knuckle fist,
slide her left hand down
her leg, bootie to boot,
crack a smile, roll her lip,
slip out to drag a cigarette.

Synthesizer choir on the blood side
of the window, bottles,
smokes, wrists, hips, third shifts
abusing that purple sun broil,
hogs, soy and corn, the hot soil
of mid-state Illinois, Christ almighty
grid roads section-by-section,
upstate above East St. Lou
deep river blues to Cairo
downstate below Centralia,
between oil pumps' slough,

drop and lift and drop
and coal fields scrape,
it was Mick spinning, sexed,
grinning, lean, cock-strutting
smoky gangster of rock and all,
tricked-out, occasionally tuxedoed,

that lick of peculiar fuck you
folk fiddle, ethereal on "Factory Girl,"
mountain whine and gypsy jam
in fiery socialist fury, skunk,
funk and shuck in a smoky joint
on her side of the river,
upright ricky-tick piano out there
past that plate glass window
where the stoplight blinked red

a slow ride gassed down,
shifting, braking, idling
low elbow sideway gaze,
no backstage pass, absolutely not
Mick, but here was the ticket,
her one-way out of Norris City.

❈ ❈ ❈

From 2008-2014, Joel Lipman was Lucas County Poet Laureate. His most recent collection is *Origins of Poetry* (RedFox Press, 2022). It's a book of visual poetry representative of another side of his work as a poet.

Lipman lives in Michigan with his wife, Cindy, and has spent practically all his years in Wisconsin, Illinois, Ohio, and Buffalo before moving to Michigan just a couple days before the state went dark during the pandemic.

Generally, he tries to write poems that fuse the people and

landscapes of the Great Lakes states. "Downstate," with a gritty, musical voice, in an orderly, ritualized pattern, does so while exploring the theme of hope.

IT DIDN'T MATTER

by Thomas Barden

It didn't matter
That he had lived without a home
Shivered in the whip wind that rolls down the river
Dodged the cops patrolling the steam plant
Dreamed about peace at the bottom of the jump
From the High-Level bridge
Found shelter at the Cherry Street Mission
Made a friend with a step van he could sleep in

It didn't matter
That one time he'd actually cried
Wondering how this could have happened
To him

What mattered was living through that
To stand with dignity on open mic night at the downtown library
And speak his poems of hope to Toledo
Accessible and beautiful, fearless and clear
To move us out of our cozy places
Down to the frozen river
To stare up at the star spangled night
To lie down in darkness
To let the bridge's rivets bruise our rib-cages
To take our turn inside his story

※ ※ ※

Thomas Barden is professor emeritus of English and former Dean of the Honors College at the University of Toledo. In retirement, he writes, teaches for the University of Toledo's Master of Liberal Studies Program, plays pickleball, and plays mandolin in an Irish music ensemble called *Toraigh an Sonas* (Gaelic for "Pursuit of Happiness").

ANOTHER ATTEMPT TO MAKE HARD-BOILED EGGS

by Sandra Rivers-Gill

When they say boil,
I think what they mean is
trouble the water.
Dress the black pot in sweat
and wild waves.

I place two raw eggs
into a small river of water.
Below the surface tension
I hear them wade and whistle like
trial and error.

So many eggs have I cracked.
This acquired taste is a seasoned dash,
a hardened meal worth
making a dish different --
no matter the cost.

Sometimes the shell wants to cling to
its own skin. I peel the fine flakes --
wash away the residue. Still

it holds to what it knows,
nothing of letting go.

I repeat the process.
To be submerged is to be changed
by what is unseen before breaking.
It isn't a cliché that a watched pot never boils.
I have witnessed this timed truth.

Eggs can be heated beyond
the hot burst of pressure.
It matters what is placed on the tongue.
It matters how it is prepared to be served.

LANDING

by Barbara Sabol

Surprised still by
his stockinged tread
up the stairs, soft
thud for a man
so large; the breadth
of his shoulders
seeming to span
every stair width;
surprised too by
his gesture's sweet
weight—removing
his shoes in the
dark so as not
to awaken
me as I lie
listening to the
white oak boards creak,
as if the house
means to settle
deeper into
its heartwood, all
the way up the
stairs his foot fall
is lit by street-

light and prospect.

AMONG THE RUINS

by LaVern Spencer McCarthy

A widow grieves alone and wonders why
an earthquake has destroyed her small estate.
Possessions disappeared and she must try
to resurrect them from the hands of fate.
Those velvet draperies she sewed with care
are shreds of blue in rubble where they fell.
One wall that held her figurines is bare.
Her husband's photograph is gone, as well.
She wonders if he watches from above
with angel tears for treasures torn apart.
A few mementos, warm with precious love
are what remain. They calm her aching heart,

for life has blessed her in a hopeful way.
She found his old love letters yesterday.

*** * * ***

Dorthy LaVern McCarthy, pen name, LaVern Spencer McCarthy, has written and published nine books, five of poetry and four of fiction.

Her work has appeared in *Writers and Readers Magazine, Meadowlark Reader, Agape Review, Fenechty Publications Anthologies Of Short Stories, From The Shadows, An Anthology*

Of Short Stories, Visions International, Fresh Words Magazine and others. She is a life member of The Poetry Society Of Texas and National Federation of State Poetry Societies, Inc.

She resides in Blair Oklahoma where she is currently writing her fifth book of short stories.

HEAVENLY CONVERSATION

by Emily Jane VandenBos Style

Six months after my mother died,
I sat across from my father
in their living room

To say out loud
that I was amiably
divorcing my long-time husband
to live with my long-time
lesbian friend

My father said
Your mother would never
have approved—
and you're going to hell

I said—this is how I think about it, Dad

If you get to heaven
before I do—
and I never show up—
it will be okay
it will be heaven

And if I get to heaven

before you do—
I promise you
when you show up
I will not say
I told you so

And I wouldn't anyway
it will be heaven

* * *

"Heavenly Conversation" was previously published in *Paterson Literary Review*.

* * *

Emily Jane VandenBos Style, who has been a teacher for more than fifty years, was raised in Kalamazoo, Michigan. She served on the Teacher Advisory Board for the first Dodge Poetry Festival in 1986 and has attended every biennial festival since. Her work has been published in the *Paterson Literary Review* and the *English Journal*. She is the Founding Co-Director of the National SEED Project, now in its 37th year, based at the Wellesley College Centers for Women. She is a grandmother of four and currently lives in the Plymouth, Massachusetts area, where her wife was raised.

AFTER THE STORM

by LaVern Spencer McCarthy

A tornado has devastated our town.
It destroyed the grain
elevator and several homes.
Tree branches and shingles
litter the streets. Trash lies everywhere.
Curtains flap through blown out
windows—pastel tongues
in a still strong wind.

Stunned people wring their hands,
gaze fearfully at each other.
Some, too old to start over,
cling to one another and weep.
All seems lost, but then the sound
of a chainsaw cuts through the air.
Clean-up has already begun.
Someone fires up a grill, 'burgers
and 'dogs for everyone.

Friends arrive to comfort and give
assistance. Laughter is heard once
more. Hope is being restored.
This is life in a small community--
neighbors helping neighbors.

CELLPHONE REACH

by Emily Jane VandenBos Style

Every time I use my cellphone to look up a word,
I think about how my father loved the dictionary—
One he kept on the shelf hidden under the wooden kitchen table
so he could pull it out even while eating
to apprehend further the taste of a specific word.
Words fueled his appetite for learning.

Another dictionary he kept in the living room
next to his easy chair where he read the newspaper,
should he need to look up an unfamiliar word
to further his comprehension.

On his bedside table lived yet another dictionary for when
he wanted to explore further a word used in a devotional.

My dad carried words in his heart
where there was always room for more—
such efficacious entities they were for him.
I hope he's carrying around a cellphone in heaven,
still expanding his vocabulary.

I WRITE THIS POEM IN THE DARK

by J. V. Sadler

I write this poem
    in the dark

Waiting for the light

    to return

THE SEA TAMER

by J. V. Sadler

Inspired by *The Awakening* by Kate Chopin

"Why does she
not float
on the water?"
asks the pointing child.

She stand alone
praying to the horizon

sweep me away
cover me
in sand and pebble

The ocean disobeys
she walks home
Alive
Disappointed,
but alive

Do women not command the sea?

❋ ❋ ❋

J. V. Sadler is a Cincinnati native and recent graduate of Oberlin College. Sadler is also a dark fiction writer and poet who focuses on societal themes. She hopes her work will inspire positive action towards consta ntly improving our world.

COOL DEFINITE

by Joseph Balaz

The open road is that way—
Start moving in that correction.

You got the memo
and you got the ammo,

so go and cross that desert
just like a determined camel.

The oasis is ahead,
where others have been led,

and with the filling water

and the earthy greens
that you will eat,

your mind will be refreshed
and fed.

That is a definition
of a cool definite,

definitely.

A HOPEFUL WORLD

by LaVern Spencer McCarthy

Since laughter was invented long ago
by someone acting in a silly way---
perhaps a caveman putting on a show---
no one can understand it in one day.
It takes a while to make a giggle tell
from where it sprang or what it holds in store.
A snicker may be secretive as well,
but later on, relent and tell us more
of what we need to know, how merriment
contrives to change our gloom into a smile.
We know a belly laugh is heaven sent
to ease our earthly sorrows for a while.

When laughter has emerged in joy and fun,
it makes a hopeful world for everyone.

RHYTHMS

by Julie Marie Hoey

I am
coral and buttercream
barefoot and running
    reaching for the sky

I am
ochre and sienna
cozy and rustling
    delivering ancient stories

I am
opalescent cobalt
reflecting and dreaming
    quilting memories with fire

I am
viridian and periwinkle
effervescent and evolving
    enchanted by light

I am
rooted and flying
earth, sunshine and water
    birthing infinite rhythms

I am
    the dawn

>   of each and every day
>   rejuvenating
>   your soul

* * *

Julie Marie Hoey is an award-winning artist and poet. Her paintings and visual work along with her poetry has been exhibited nationally and lives in collections worldwide. She likes to say she is an artist, writer, teacher - poet and believer. When painting and writing Julie Marie feels possibility. She listens to the paint and rhythm of the words. She lets her brush or pen guide her. Julie Marie looks for the heart of the matter that she isn't always aware of until in the act of creating Her mind begins the journey. Her soul, brush and pen complete it. Julie Marie loves belly laughs, storytelling, vibrant colors, gardening, her cat Jasper Johns, good grammar, interesting words, reading, fixing things, exercising and yoga. She is certain her greatest gift is amusing others—unintentionally.

GATHA

by John Burroughs

When I sit on my bunk
I vow to all beings
that I will see the beauty in my blanket
and the cold.

IN THE WAKE

by John Burroughs

Driving through the last of Ian's tears
from Frostburg's hazel-eyed dazzle
to Cincinnati's queen city sizzle
my mind can't help careening backwards
to Maryland where from clatter to clatter
through book boxes, diner provisions,
Leftist brews and punk poet chatter
I dreamed and continue to dream
of an open window, a brown sash wet
with whatever might matter and yearn
to both return and proceed, dancing
together in the burgeoning whether.

CLEANSE

by Julie Marie Hoey

> *In honor of my maternal grandmother, Florence McNamara Pendergast, who asked the question, "What does the ocean heal?" Her answer was, "Everything."*

those tears I shed were clear
streams running down the mountainside
tumbling over clay and stone
through woods, drifting over
grasses in the morning mist
        curving, careening, caressing

catching sunlight; refracting rubies, sapphires, ambers and opals
water carrying copper, crystals,
clay and quartz; strong and supple
        serenading, sunshine and solace

kissing Mother Earth as she settles
into another sleepy morning
brooking through dells and vales
past farms, springing into and under
ravines reaching for a river
that joins another and another
        miraculously, masterfully and mightily

announcing intention broadly
to towns thoughtful, through cities stark
filling swamps, bays and quarries
arriving at the Atlantic in March
        daring, deliberate and deep

mingling with the Pacific in August
inviting all to swim her waters
float buoyantly in the salt
to wade through worries
        whisper, wonder and worship
at the ocean; any of the seven seas
toes bury themselves in silt and guide
children building castles in the sand
and past the crashing waves
surfers ride her undulations
families and friends foster
        ferment, forge, forgive

via shoreline walks and winks
sunbathing, precocious poses
a frisbee toss, knowing glances and conversations through sunglasses
building relationships that
        reverberate, reveal and rejuvenate

in waters
that cleanse the soul
in waters
that mend all that's hurting
        holding each other
                heralding each other

>healing
>>each other

BOOKS BY THIS AUTHOR

Mad As Hell: An Anthology Of Angry Poetry; Edited With An Introduction By J. R. Simons

"Mad as Hell" is a collection of angry poems by some of the nation's finest new, emerging, and established poets, including Mariana Goycoechea, John Burroughs, Kenneth Hickey, Debbie Allen, Lynne Bronstein, Joe Balaz, Laura Grace Wledon, Kelly Boyer Sagert, Alex Gildzen, Randy C. White, Thomas Barden, R. T. Castleberry, J. R. Simons, Tabassam Shah, and Jason Franklin Blakely.

The Naked Truth: Poems By J. R. Simons

This is J. R. Simons' second collection of poetry.

Streetlight Sonata: Poems By J. R. Simons

This is J. R. Simons' multiple award winning first collection of poetry.

Rattle & Numb: Selected And New Poems, 1992-2019 By John Burroughs

"Rattle & Numb" is the prestige edition of the poetry of John Burroughs, State of Ohio Beat Poet Laureate 2019-2021, and master of the expressive beat voice for which he has toured the US in his evangelism.

Pidgin Eye By Joseph Balaz

"Pidgin Eye" features thirty-five years of poetry by acclaimed author Joe Balaz. Writing in Pidgin (Hawai'i Creole English), he honors the beauty, strength, and complexity of Hawai'i and the voices of its peoples. Balaz's philosophical lyricism tightly weaves history and humor, aloha 'āina and protest, the spiritual and the everyday. Together, these poems envision a world in which—like Pidgin—"everyting deserves to fly." Joe Balaz, born and raised in Wahiawa on the island of O'ahu, is of Hawaiian, Slovakian, and Irish ancestry. He is the author of multiple books of poetry in Standard English and Pidgin (Hawai'i Creole English), as well as the editor of Ho'omānoa: An Anthology of Contemporary Hawaiian Literature. His writing, visual poetry, and artwork have been published in national and international journals and anthologies. Throughout his career, he has passionately advocated for Hawaiian and Pidgin literature.

Crimson Sunshine By Jessica Weyer Bentley

Since losing her father when Jessica was 5 years old, words have soothed her soul. At 9, she began penning the words in her head onto paper as poetry and prose, and continued penning through college, work, and raising two children. Her writing has earned awards and been published in the newspaper and the award-winning "Grief Diaries" book series. Paired for the first time with her daughter's illustrations, "Crimson Sunshine" is an introduction to Jessica's poetry that stems from a life lived with great lows and ultimate highs as seen through the eyes of both a young 5-year-old girl and survivor of astounding loss and accomplished mother.

Sharing This Delicate Bread, Barbara Sabol, Editor

Through these pages, the broad swath of relationships that

bind us to family, to lovers, to childhood memories, to the natural world, and to our wounded society are enacted through distinctive imagery and voice. The reader is invited to delve into a profound truth: "the world is just as beautiful as it's hurt" ("Crivelli's Madonna and Child," George Franklin). Taken together, the work highlights the vital role of poetry to affirm our shared, keenly lived experiences as we come together at a common table to share the "delicate bread" signified in Seth Jani's beautiful poem, "Repast."

South Shore Suite...Poems By J C Sulzenko

South Shore Suite...POEMS (2017) offers a selection of narrative and lyric poems arranged in four sections. The eponymous "South Shore Suite" emerged from JC's posting a line of poetry a day on her blog for a year. "Second Nature" focuses a wider lens on the natural world. "Cameo Appearances" draws poems from interviews JC conducted with people in different professions about life choices they made. The final section, "Cradle to Grave," contains poems closest to JC's personal experience. Copies available through www.jcsulzenko.com.

Bricolage, A Gathering Of Centos By A. Garnett Weiss

Published by Aelous House under her pseudonym, A. Garnett Weiss, Bricolage, A Gathering of Centos is JC Sulzenko's first collection of centos: found poems using other poet's lines to create a new work, independent in form and meaning from its sources. Among 5 finalists for the national 2022 Fred Kerner Book Award from the Canadian Authors Association, Bricolage contains award-winning poetry that "resounds with the echo of greatness, finely chiseled into a composition, a recomposition, a deposition on the value of recurrence. They signal a new way to read the world and find rich golden veins in borrowed words." (A quote from Gregory Betts, author of Psychic Geographies and Other Topics). Copies available through www.jcsulzenko.com

Origins Of Poetry By Joel Lipman

A collection of small artists' books dedicated to experimental, concrete and visual poetry, or any work combining text and visual arts in the spirit of dada or fluxus.

Made in the USA
Middletown, DE
03 December 2023